To my Charlie Mae, my world changer.
Your ability to change lives far outshines any disability, my love.
You have shown me realms of joy I never knew existed.
Keep shining, beautiful girl. Mama loves you.

Charlie Mae's First Day

# Charlie Mae's First Day

By Hannah Wilson

Illustrated by Kim Soderberg

Hey, I'm Charlie Mae.
And I'm so excited for school today!

I've got my backpack and my cutest clothes.
We're almost there. Here we go!

There's my classroom, right over there!
I'm going in, it's okay if they stare.

I'm a bit different, you can probably see.
So, let me tell you a little more about me.

I can't walk like you but that doesn't get me down.
I have a chair with wheels that helps me around.

I don't use words but can listen with my ears.

You can sing me a song, I would love to hear.

Although I have a mouth, that's not how I eat my food.
I have something special, it's called a g-tube.

My lunch comes through my tube
and goes straight into my tummy.
Even though I can't taste it, I'll bet you it is yummy.

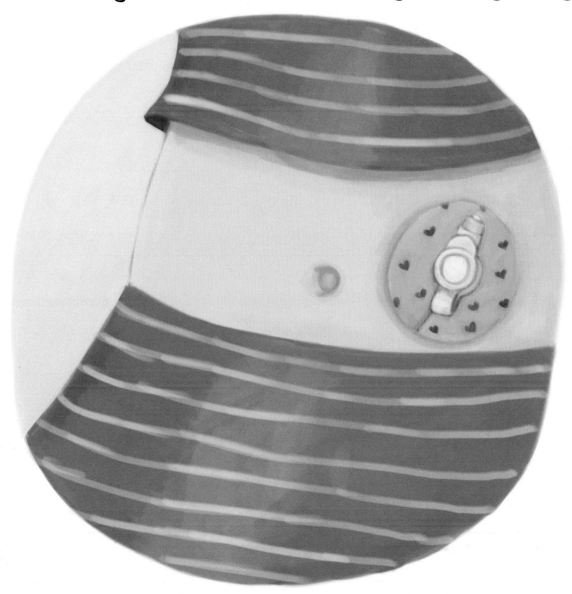

I may have a seizure, no need to be scared.
I could shake and get sleepy, but the teacher's prepared.

I've had epilepsy since I was 3 months old.
That's why I have seizures, so I was told.

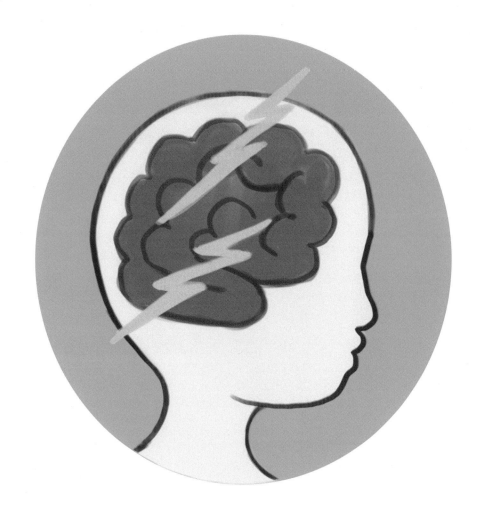

Seizures are like a lightning storm inside of my brain.
They make me really tired and feel oh so drained.

After a short nap I'll be a-okay!
Don't worry, I'll be fine and ready in time to play.

Why? You ask, do you have all these problems.
My mama says they're what makes me so awesome.

Simply put, I was born this way.
That's how God made me, my parents say.

I'm still a kid, a kid just like you.
And most times I like the same things you do.

On nice cool days I like to play outside.
I love to swing and go on wagon rides.

I have a red tricycle, come over and we'll race!

Don't forget your helmet, it's good to be safe.

I want to play ball and take lessons for dance.

And one day I will, when I have the chance.

I love the color pink and my special baby doll.

She looks just like me, with a wheelchair and all!

I have a sister at home, 3 dogs too!

And I love cartoons. Tell me about you.

Thank you, new friend, for being so kind.

Even though we are different, I sure don't mind.

With you as my pal, I can't go wrong.
I know we'll be buddies all year long.

The End

Residing in Alabama, Hannah Wilson is a wife and proud mother
to her growing family. She delights in her role as a stay-at-home mom
and fully embraces life as a special needs parent.
Her oldest daughter, Charlie, was born with a rare genetic mutation
that causes severe developmental delays and intractable epilepsy.

Hannah is a member of the Kids Crew Leadership Council
of the Epilepsy Foundation of America, serving as a voice
for Charlie and other kids alike.

Through her book, Hannah hopes to increase awareness
around children with different abilities, all while
spreading joy to other families like her own.

*Let's stay in touch!* Find us on social media at
***www.Facebook.com/charliemaesfirstday***
and Instagram ***@charliemaesfirstday***

Ohio based Children's Book Illustrator, Kim Soderberg has been working as a professional in the industry for the past ten years. She is known for her use of bright color, endearing characters and rich environments.

She is also a wife and mother to three energetic children, who give her constant inspiration. Her middle son, Grady, has a diagnosis of Autism Spectrum Disorder. As a special needs mom herself, Kim jumped at the opportunity to work with Hannah on "Charlie Mae's First Day."

Kim is a member of SCBWI and some of her clients include Scholastic, Creative Teaching Press, National Geographic, Animal Tales and Girls World Magazine.

Kim is represented by Illustration Online LLC.